Dear Parent:
Your child's love of reading starts here!

Every child learns to read in a different way and at his or her own speed. Some go back and forth between reading levels and read favorite books again and again. Others read through each level in order. You can help your young reader improve and become more confident by encouraging his or her own interests and abilities. From books your child reads with you to the first books he or she reads alone, there are I Can Read Books for every stage of reading:

SHARED READING
Basic language, word repetition, and whimsical illustrations, ideal for sharing with your emergent reader

BEGINNING READING
Short sentences, familiar words, and simple concepts for children eager to read on their own

READING WITH HELP
Engaging stories, longer sentences, and language play for developing readers

READING ALONE
Complex plots, challenging vocabulary, and high-interest topics for the independent reader

I Can Read Books have introduced children to the joy of reading since 1957. Featuring award-winning authors and illustrators and a fabulous cast of beloved characters, I Can Read Books set the standard for beginning readers.

A lifetime of discovery begins with the magical words "I Can Read!"

Visit www.icanread.com for information
on enriching your child's reading experience.

I Can Read® and I Can Read Book® are trademarks of HarperCollins Publishers.

My Little Pony: Izzy Does It
MY LITTLE PONY TM & © 2022 Hasbro.
All rights reserved. Printed in the United States of America.
No part of this book may be used or reproduced in any manner whatsoever without written permission except
in the case of brief quotations embodied in critical articles and reviews.
For information address HarperCollins Children's Books, a division of HarperCollins Publishers,
195 Broadway, New York, NY 10007.
www.icanread.com

Library of Congress Control Number: 2022938171
ISBN 978-0-06-303757-1
Book design by Stephanie Hays

22 23 24 25 26 LBM 10 9 8 7 6 5 4 3 2 1   ❖   First Edition

IZZY DOES IT

Based on the episode by Jim Martin
Adapted by Alexandra West

HARPER
An Imprint of HarperCollinsPublishers

One beautiful day in Maretime Bay,

Izzy was building a birthday tower

of friendship for Sunny.

She was wearing her crafting glasses.

Izzy was super creative.

She liked to make cool things

from what she found.

But suddenly her tower shook

and fell over!

5

"Nooo!" Izzy shouted.

Her friends Hitch and Zipp

saw the crash and ran to help.

Izzy was disappointed.

Her birthday tower of friendship

for Sunny was destroyed.

Frustrated, Izzy kicked it.

That sent a big mess into the air.

Izzy caught a sparkly bracelet.

"An accidentally awesome accessory!"
she said.

"Izzy, are you okay?" Sunny asked.
The friends turned to see Sunny
coming from the Crystal Brighthouse.
"I heard a bang."

"I'm okay!" Izzy shouted.

"Happy Birthday, Sunny!"

Izzy presented Sunny

with the sparkly accessory.

"I can't wait to show this off," Sunny said.

"I'm selling smoothies
at the Craft Fair.

Do you want to come?"

"Of course!" Izzy said excitedly.

When Sunny and Izzy arrived,

they couldn't believe their eyes.

There were so many crafts to see!

Just then, they saw their friend Pipp talking to her social media followers. "The Craft Fair is the only place for the hottest crafts!" she said.

"What is that?!" Pipp shouted.
Pipp was pointing to the
accessory in Sunny's mane.

Pipp pulled out her phone again. "Come to the Craft Fair and get an Izzy original creation!" she said. "Well, but it was sort of . . . one of a kind," Izzy said.

Suddenly Pipp's followers
swarmed the pony friends.
They all wanted an Izzy original!

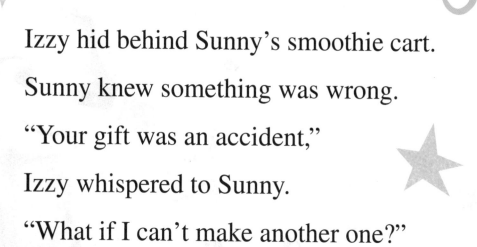

Izzy hid behind Sunny's smoothie cart.

Sunny knew something was wrong.

"Your gift was an accident,"
Izzy whispered to Sunny.

"What if I can't make another one?"

"Everything you make is great!"
Sunny said.

Suddenly Pipp popped her head in.

"Just let your creativity fly," Pipp said.

"Do what you did and make it better!"

18

Izzy knew her friends were right.

She headed back to the

Crystal Brighthouse to start crafting.

Izzy had everything she needed.

"Okay, now it's time to make something even better than Sunny's gift."

A while later, Pipp came in to check on her.

"This isn't going very well," Izzy said.

"You need inspiration," Pipp said.

"Grab your stuff.

We're going to find customers!"

After a lot of hard work,

Izzy finally managed to get

all her art supplies to the Craft Fair.

Izzy began to jam things together.

Izzy created a new accessory. "Ta-da!" she said, giving it to a fan. "This isn't the same as the thing you made earlier," the pony said, disappointed.

Sunny spotted Izzy
among the pile of supplies.
"I don't know what I'm doing,"
Izzy said to Sunny.

Later that day, Sunny went back

Sunny put her hoof on Izzy's shoulder.
"Inspiration comes from who you are.
You need to go back to your roots."
"That's it!" Izzy shouted.

Later that day, Sunny went back
to the Crystal Brighthouse.
She found a note from Izzy that said:
"I couldn't create good crafts so
I went back to Bridlewood for good."

"Oh, no!" Sunny said.

"Izzy left Maretime Bay forever!"

Sunny gathered the pony friends.

"This is all my fault!" Pipp said.

"No, this is my fault," Sunny said.

"I told her to go back to her roots."

"Oh, hi guys," Izzy said.

"Izzy!" Sunny shouted.

"Didn't you read my note?" Izzy asked.

"'I went back to Bridlewood for good

. . . art supplies,'" Izzy said.

Sunny just hadn't turned over the note.

"Sunny and Pipp taught me
that to be creative,
I just need to be myself!
So I went back to get this."
It was an amazing craft cart!

"Presenting . . . Izzy Does It!" Izzy said.
"It has everything I need to make
something that's totally me!"